Grandpappy
Snippy Snappies

by Lynn Plourde

illustrated by
Christopher Santoro

HarperCollinsPublishers

Grandpappy snippy snappies
His suspenders all the day
Snippy-snappy-snoo
What those suspenders can do!

Snippy snappy **up**
Snippy snappy **down**
Snippy snappy smile
Snippy snappy frown
Snippy-snappy-snoo

Grandpappy hears a
MOO! MOO!

Wayward cows
Are stuck
In some muck
So Grandpappy gives a snap
To get the cows unstuck

Raining milk
From Kansas City to
Kalamazoo

Grandpappy snippy snappies
His suspenders all the day
Snippy-snappy-snoo
What those suspenders can do!

Snippy snappy **left**
Snippy snappy *right*
Snippy snappy l o o s e
Snippy snappy tight
Snippy-snappy-snoo

Grandpappy hears a

woo! woo!

The sheriff's car
Turns the wrong way
Crashes into some bales of hay
So Grandpappy gives a snap
To send the sheriff on his way

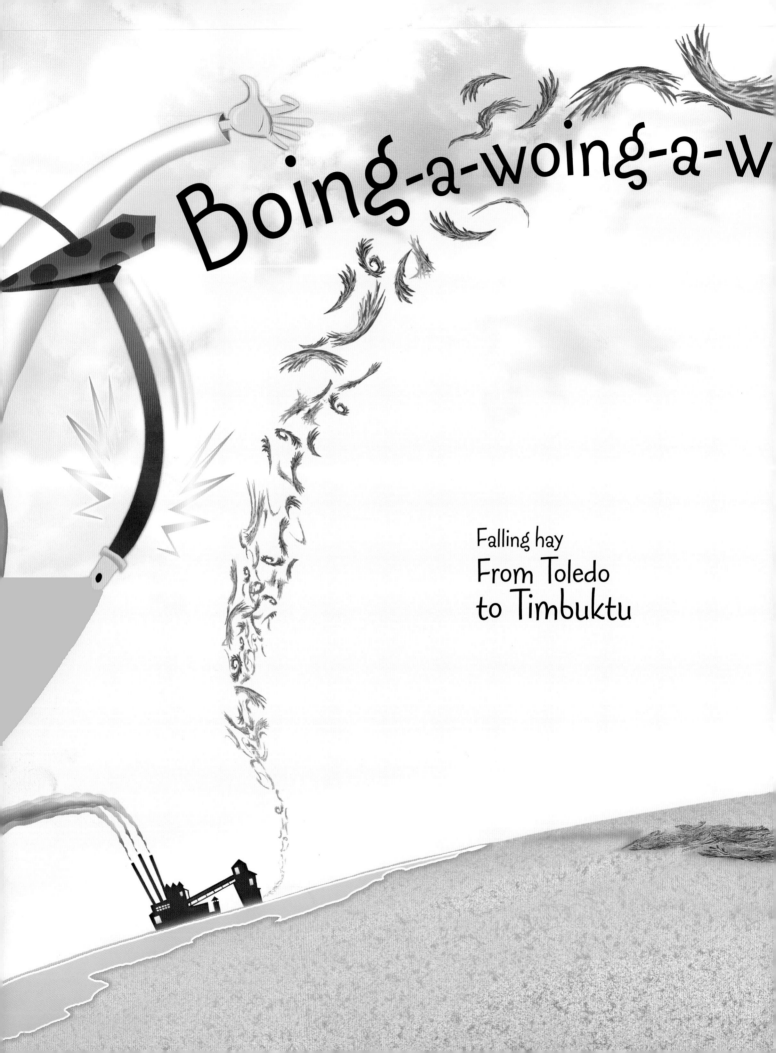

Boing-a-woing-a-w

Falling hay
From Toledo
to Timbuktu

OOOOOOOOOOO

Grandpappy snippy snappies
His suspenders all the day
Snippy-snappy-snoo
What those suspenders can do!

Snippy snappy *fast*
Snippy snappy s l o w
Snippy snappy **STOP**
Snippy snappy................GO
Snippy-snappy-snoo
Grandpappy hears a

CHOO! CHOO!

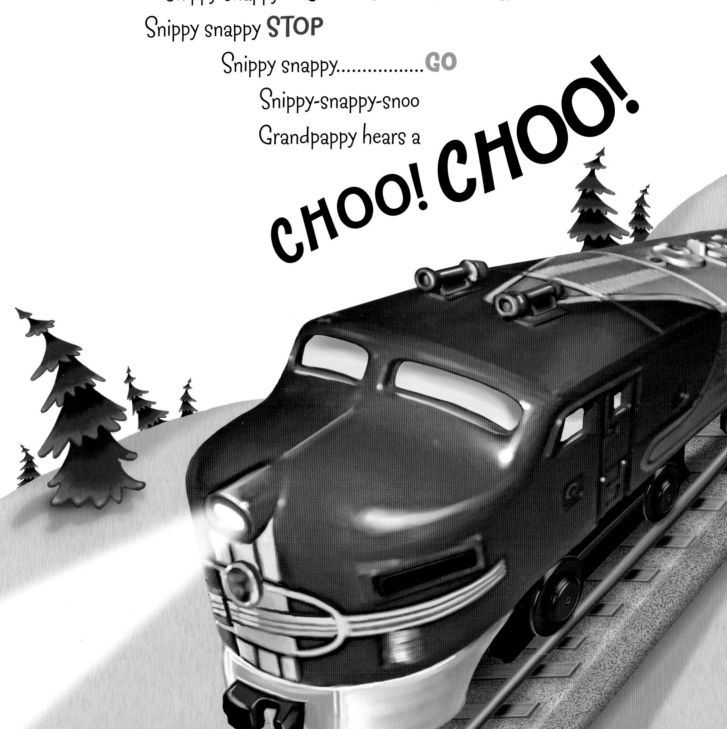

The mail train
Derails from the track
Even the caboose way up back
So Grandpappy gives a snap
To get the train on track

Boing-a-choing-a-chooo

Rushing mail
from Mars
to the moon

Grandpappy snippy snappies
His suspenders all the day
Snippy-snappy-snoo

Boing-

a-

droing-

a-

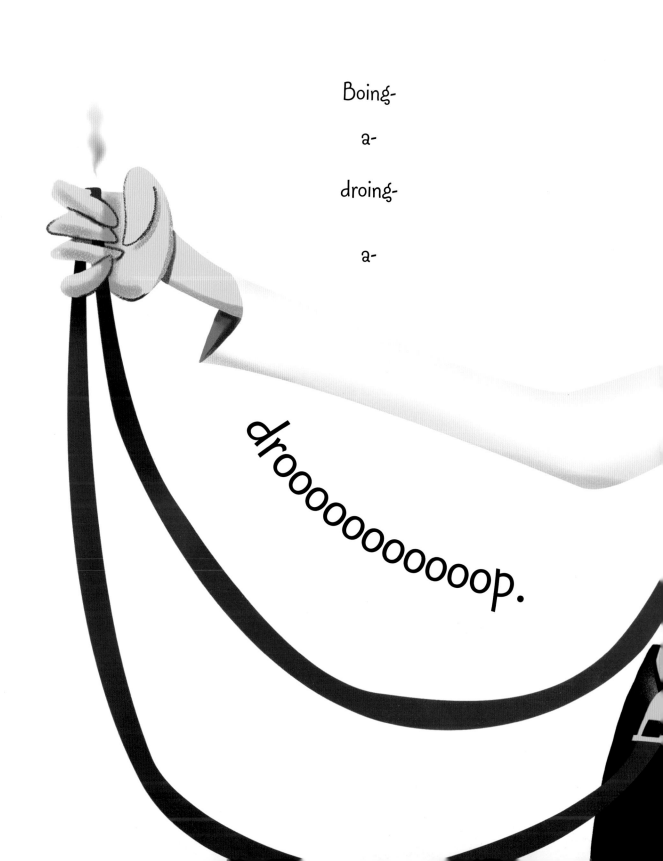

drooooooooooop.

Caw!
Caw!

A flock of crows
Takes Grandmammy by the dress
Starts to fly away
Grandmammy's in distress
So she yells, "Grandpappy, dear,

Snappy to
and
get
me
down
from
here."

"Yoo hoo,
My honey poo,
Without suspenders
What can I do?"

Nevertheless

Grandpappy tries
To rescue Grandmammy
'Fore the crows do fly

DASH!

LEAP!

DROP!

Caw-a-caw-a-coooo

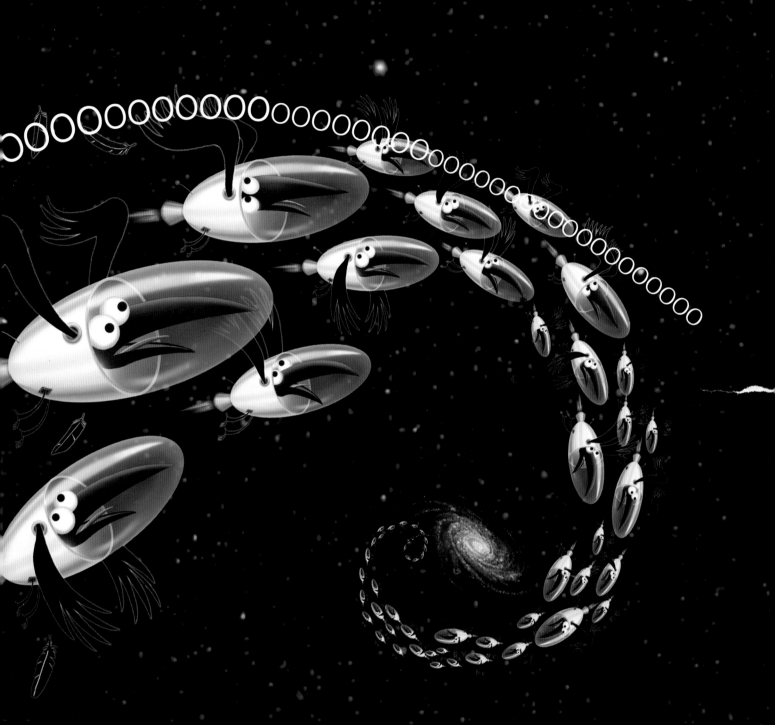

Flying feathers
From Earth
to Galaxy 42

Grandpappy's a hero
No suspenders in sight
He used his own pair of bloomers
To save his wife

Smoochy-smacky-
smoooooooooooooooooo!

What that
GRANDPAPPY
can do!

With love and thanks to Lawrence and Charlene,
for being the best in-laws
and a great grandpappy and grandmammy
—L.P.

For Valerie
—C.S.

Library of Congress Cataloging-in-Publication Data
Plourde, Lynn.
Grandpappy snippy snappies / by Lynn Plourde ; illustrated by Christopher Santoro.
p.   cm.
Summary: When things go wrong around his farm Grandpappy sets them right with a snap of his
suspenders, but Grandmammy is in trouble and the suspenders are all worn out.
ISBN 978-0-06-028050-5 (trade bdg.) — ISBN 978-0-06-029528-8 (lib. bdg.)
[1. Farmers—Fiction. 2. Clothing and dress—Fiction. 3. Humorous stories.
4. Stories in rhyme.] I. Santoro, Christopher, ill. II. Title.
PZ8.3.P5586922 Gr 2006 2001024328 [E]—dc21
Designed by Stephanie Bart-Horvath
1 2 3 4 5 6 7 8 9 10
❖
First Edition